Bargaining at the Market

Written by Margaret MacDonald

Picture Dictionary

buyers and sellers

floating market

flea market

stalls

A market is a place where people go to buy and sell goods.
People can buy and sell many things at markets.

Bargaining

In most markets,
goods do not have set prices.
The buyer asks how much something is.
The seller tells the buyer a price.
The buyer says a lower price.
The seller says a price
that is higher
than the price the buyer said.
Buyers and sellers
talk about the price
until they agree
what the buyer will pay.
This is called bargaining.

These buyers and sellers are bargaining at a food market in Ecuador.

Markets around the World

There are markets in most countries around the world.

But not all markets are the same. Some markets sell only one thing.

Some markets sell only birds.
Other markets sell only clothes.
Some markets sell only fish.
Other markets sell only spices.
Some markets sell only meat.
Other markets sell only vegetables.

This market sells only fish.

Some markets sell many things.
Some of these things are old.
Some of these things are new.
Markets that sell old and new things
are called flea markets.
Sometimes they are called
swap meets.

In some countries,
markets that sell old and new things
are called bazaars.

This flea market sells old and new things.

Some markets are inside.
Some markets are outside.
Some markets have stalls inside
and stalls outside.
Sometimes the outside stalls
are not covered.
Sometimes the outside stalls
look like tents.
The tents shade people
and the goods they sell.
Some markets have little shops
as well as stalls.
Some of these markets are very big.
They have hundreds of stalls and stores.
Some of these markets are very small.
They have just a few stalls.

This market has stalls inside as well as outside.

Some markets are called
floating markets.
People buy and sell things from boats
at floating markets.
People also buy and sell things
from stalls on the riverbank.
Some markets are open
one or two days a week.
Some markets are open every day.

Floating market in Thailand

Some people go to markets every day.
They go to buy goods.
They go to sell goods.
They go to swap goods.
They bargain to get the best price
for the goods
they are buying or selling.

What Will You Find at Markets?

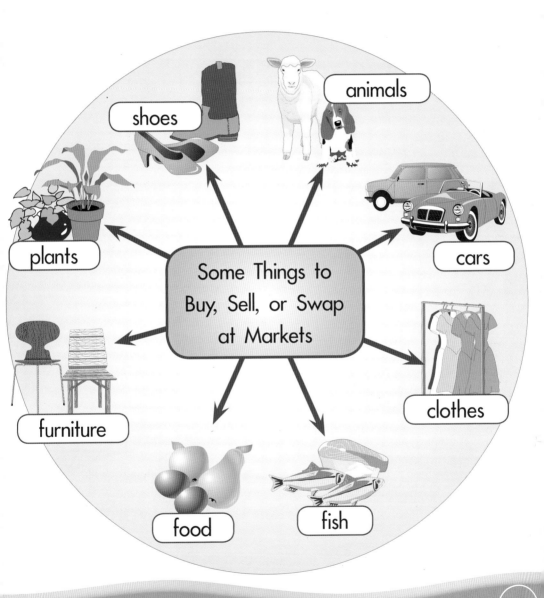

shoes

animals

cars

clothes

fish

food

furniture

plants

Some Things to Buy, Sell, or Swap at Markets

Activity Page

1. Draw a market with people bargaining.

2. Label –
   - The buyer
   - The seller
   - The stall
   - The goods the seller is selling

3. Write a sentence that tells more about the market.

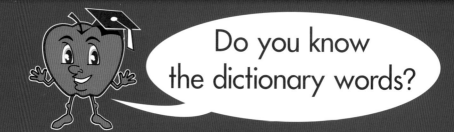

Do you know the dictionary words?